# Lucy Comes to Stay

# Lucy
# Comes to Stay

*Rosemary Wells* PAINTINGS BY *Mark Graham*

Dial Books for Young Readers  *New York*

Published by Dial Books for Young Readers
A Division of Penguin Books USA Inc.
375 Hudson Street
New York, New York 10014

Designed by Nancy R. Leo
Printed in the U.S.A.
First Edition
1 3 5 7 9 10 8 6 4 2

Library of Congress Cataloging in Publication Data
Wells, Rosemary.
Lucy comes to stay / Rosemary Wells; paintings by Mark Graham—1st ed.
p.   cm.
Summary: Mary Elizabeth loves her new puppy Lucy, but discovers
that puppies need special care and understanding.
ISBN 0-8037-1213-8 (trade).—ISBN 0-8037-1214-6 (library)
[1. Dogs—Fiction.   2. Animals—Infancy—Fiction.]
I. Graham, Mark, ill.   II. Title.
PZ7.W46843Lu 1994   [E]—dc20   91-15779   CIP   AC

*The art for each picture consists of an oil painting that is color-separated
and reproduced in full color.*

## Kissing Lessons

The day we brought Lucy home she was so tiny she could have fit in my mother's coat pocket. I held her on my lap. She was warm, but she shivered at the noises in the street and the hum of the car motor. On top of my legs her feet were as light as cloud feet.

"Lucy," I whispered, "I love you and will keep you safe and not let anything hurt you."

"Mary Elizabeth, what did you whisper to Lucy?" my mother asked.

"It's a secret," I answered.

Lucy had never seen grass. She had never been outdoors at night. She had never been in a house. My father is very big, and I thought she'd be afraid of him. But when we brought her in the door, Daddy dropped right down on the carpet and let her kiss his face all over. When Lucy kissed Daddy, she nibbled his ears and nose with her sharp puppy teeth.

"Lucy needs kissing lessons," said Daddy.

## Lucy's First Night

I wanted Lucy to sleep in my bed.

"She'll be cold and lonely at night," I told my mother.

"When she's older, then maybe," said my mother. "When she can be clean all night long in your room, then she may sleep there. Until then she has her own sleeping box that she can see out of, with a door that closes and a soft towel."

"It isn't her own box," I grumped at my mother. "It's Bernadette's crate. It even has Bernadette's name on it." Bernadette was my grandma's collie.

"I don't think Lucy can read yet," said my mother.

BERNADETTE

Late that night Lucy cried. I woke up. Lucy needs me, I thought, but I did promise not to take her in my bed.

Lucy cried more. Bernadette is a big collie, I said to myself. As big as Lucy and me put together. And I certainly didn't promise not to get into Lucy's bed!

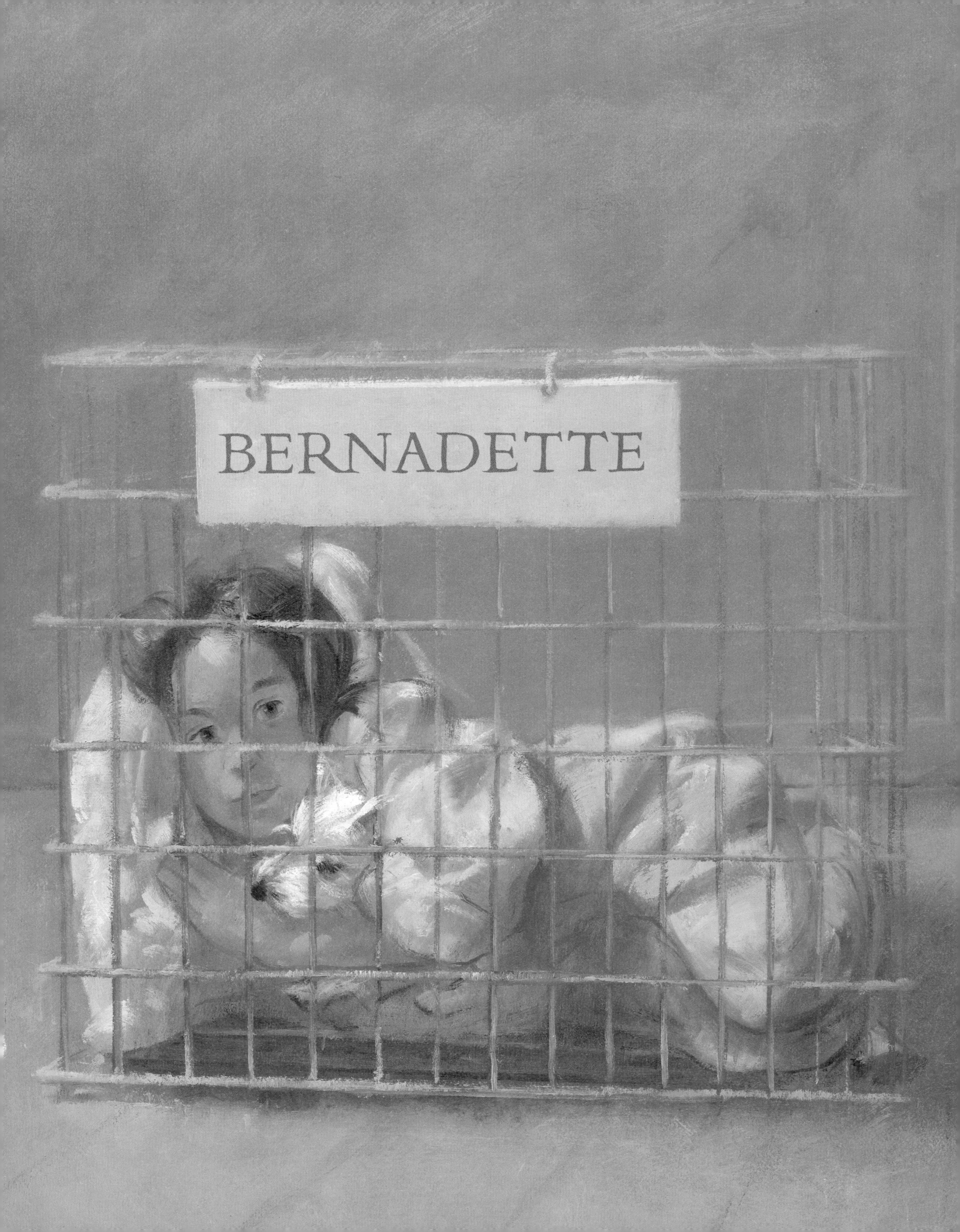
BERNADETTE

## Lucy's Bad Day

Lucy had a bad day. It started in the morning when she got sick. "She must have eaten some sticks in the garden," said my mother, who was about to mop up after Lucy. I was ready to put on my brand-new leather-laced moccasins for school. I looked down on the floor.

"Oh, no!" I said. "Those aren't sticks. Those are chewed bits of my leather laces that Lucy just threw up, and I can't wear my new shoes without them. And my last year's shoes are thrown away!"

Even though I had to go to school that morning wearing two-year-old loafers, Lucy was too sick to scold.

I stuffed my pillow into her crate and wedged myself in just enough so Lucy could sleep with me around her. Lucy went right to sleep on my pillow. When pins and needles attacked me, I had to leave. I tiptoed back to my own bed. Pillowless, I watched the stars out my window until my eyes just closed by themselves.

When I got back from school, Lucy had found a ballpoint pen. She had chewed through it, and her beard and feet were blue. I had to give her a bath so she wouldn't get indelible ink all over everything. Lucy hated her bath, but she was too blue to scold.

That night she walked around and around the bathtub rim as I sat in my bubbles. Suddenly she slipped in. She did not like the bubbles or the hot water. She did not like holding still for another toweling off. But she was too tired to scold.

"Lucy," I said, "tomorrow is another day."

## Two Things at Once

Lucy loved to lie on a certain spot on the rug where she got hot from the sun. Then she needed water. When she was very sleepy and very thirsty, she tried to drink lying down.

"That is impossible, Lucy," I said. "You can only do one thing at a time. Drink or lie down, but you can't do both."

She tried again though. This time she sat and stretched her neck to see if she could drink while sitting down.

"Lucy," I said, "stand and drink!"

Lucy fell asleep standing up.

## Home Remedies

Lucy had rumbles in her tummy. "She sounds like a fish aquarium," I said to my father.

"Try and see if she'll eat anything," said Daddy.

I looked in the liver treat jar. All the treats were gone, and at the bottom was only a brown dust.

Daddy put her breakfast food in her dish. Lucy wouldn't eat it. He offered her a piece of buttered toast. Lucy wouldn't eat it. Then he tried a spoon of ice cream. Lucy wouldn't eat it.

"Wait, Daddy," I said. "I know what she'll eat." I made a special mixture using just a teaspoon of vanilla ice cream. Lucy ate it all up and her tummy was quiet immediately.

"Whatever did you put in that ice cream?" asked Daddy.

"Liver dust," I said. "Liver ice cream is her favorite flavor."

## Together at Last

One freezing, stormy night when Lucy was just six months old, I cleared off the whole dinner table by myself. I washed all the dishes and dried them, brushed the crumbs off the table, and put everything back in the icebox.

Then I sat down and waited for my mother to notice me.

"Mary Elizabeth," she said, "I think you want something."

"Ma," I said, "you know what?"

"What?" she said.

"At night I worry," I said.

"What on earth do you have to be worried about?" she asked.

"Everything," I answered. "Sometimes I think there's an invisible worrier who comes and sits on my bed and worries me."

"Well, what are we going to do to stop you from worrying?" asked my mother.

"If Lucy were next to me, she would keep the worrier away," I said.

My mother fussed with the sleeve of her dress. She straightened the slipcover on the arm of her chair. She closed the book on her lap and adjusted the bookmark. "Well, maybe just for tonight," she said.

Lucy had her own pillow next to mine. I whispered to her that she would have to be very good or we wouldn't be allowed to do this again. We listened to a pine branch blow against the window, and fell asleep to the lullaby of the rain.